*A ma Grand-mère*
—V. Van den Abeele

Text © 2006 Véronique Van den Abeele; Illustrations © 2006 Claude K. Dubois
Published in 2007 by Eerdmans Books for Young Readers, an imprint of Wm. B. Eerdmans Publishing Co.

Wm. B. Eerdmans Publishing Co.
2140 Oak Industrial Dr NE, Grand Rapids, Michigan 49505
P.O. Box 163, Cambridge CB3 9PU U.K.

www.eerdmans.com/youngreaders
First published by Mijade in Belgium in 2006

Manufactured in Belgium

07 08 09 10 11 12 13   8 7 6 5 4 3 2 1

**Library of Congress Cataloging-in-Publication Data**
Van den Abeele, Véronique
[Ma grand-mere Alzha– quoi? English]
Still My Grandma / written by Véronique Van den Abeele ; illustrated by Claude K. Dubois.
p. cm.
Summary: A young girl describes her special relationship with her grandmother, both before and after Grandma contracts Alzheimer's disease.
ISBN 978-0-8028-5323-3 (alk. paper)
[1. Grandmothers–Fiction.  2. Alzheimer's disease–Fiction.] I. Dubois, Claude K., ill.  II. Title.
PZ7.A158937For 2007
[E]–dc22
2006025265

Matthew Van Zomeren, graphic designer

# Still My Grandma

Written by Véronique Van den Abeele

Illustrated by Claude K. Dubois

Eerdmans Books for Young Readers

Grand Rapids, Michigan · Cambridge, U.K.

I've known Grandma my whole life. I know a lot of things about her, almost as many as I know about Mom and Dad. And Grandma knows everything about me, like that September is my favorite month and that I can eat three whole hot dogs for dinner.

Before I went to school, I could have sleepovers at Grandma's any night of the week. Mom would walk me up to the door, and Grandma would watch at the window. She always pretended she didn't know who I was.

"Is that the mailman?" she would ask in a loud voice.

But then she would open the door laughing and scoop me up in a big hug. "My sweet Camille!" she would say into my ear.

Her house always smelled good, like strawberry jam and warm bread.

Grandma and I had our own special traditions. First, we looked in her treasure box at the tiny spoons, teacups, and glittery necklaces. Then we would look at old pictures. My favorite is one of Grandma when she was my age, all bundled up in a winter coat, sitting on a sled.

"Is that really you, Grandma?" I would ask her every time. "It looks exactly like me!"

Then we would go out shopping. At the grocery store Grandma would let me get a piece of candy at the checkout. I always let her hold my hand, even though I'm too old for that.

Grandma liked getting fresh air, so we would take the
long way home, through the park to the duck pond.

We liked to throw pieces of bread to the ducks and watch them fight over the food. We would quack at each other the rest of the way home, giggling.

Sometimes we pretended to be famous television chefs. I was the star and Grandma was my assistant. Our specialty was chocolate cupcakes with lots of frosting. We wore aprons and talked in funny accents. Our cupcakes were my favorite!

When she tucked me into bed, Grandma would tell stories about when she was a little girl. She had five sisters and five brothers and she was the youngest. Even though her family was poor, Grandma said she always had fun because her brothers and sisters loved to play games and spoil her with attention.

Right before we said goodnight, we would give each other our special "loud smacking kiss." We laughed so hard we thought we might wake the neighbors!

I never wanted Grandma to leave, so I'd ask her to sing me a song to put me to sleep. She would rub my head as she sang all the verses to "You Are My Sunshine."

Then, a few months ago, Grandma started acting different.

"Good morning, Susan!" she said when I came over one day.

"Grandma! You know my name is Camille," I said, laughing.

I thought she was just pretending to be funny.

But later, when I asked to see her treasure box, she looked me straight in the eye and said, "Come on, Daddy, let's go fishing." I knew she wasn't pretending this time. She was confused. I didn't want to make her feel bad, so I didn't say anything.

A few weeks later, we were getting ready to bake cupcakes, and I saw Grandma open the fridge. I thought she was getting out the ingredients. But I saw her put her shoes on the shelf right next to the milk!

"What are you doing?" I asked.

Grandma got a funny look on her face. All she said was, "Silly me!"

That night Grandma wasn't confused when she was telling stories about when she was a little girl. But the next morning at breakfast, Grandma poured orange juice on my cereal.

Something was wrong, and I was worried.

We found out that Grandma was sick, but not the kind
where you cough and blow your nose.

"She has Alzheimer's disease," the doctor said.

My mom says that's what makes her do strange things.

"But how can she get better?" I asked my mom.

"She won't. You have to love Grandma the way she is."

I don't have sleepovers with Grandma anymore. Now she lives in a big house with lots of grandmas and grandpas like her.

Nurses take care of Grandma because she needs help washing her hair, getting dressed, and going for walks. Grandma doesn't have her own kitchen, just a bedroom, so we can't bake chocolate cupcakes anymore.

I am sad that Grandma has changed so much, but I know that she is sick and she can't help it. And the doctor said the best thing to do is to visit, so I come with Mom and Dad every Saturday.

And you know what? Even though most times Grandma forgets my name, we still have our traditions. Mom and I bake chocolate cupcakes at home, and I bring Grandma the one with the most frosting.

When we go for walks, I'm the one who tells stories to Grandma. I talk about my friends from school, and I bring my own treasures, like the bright red leaf I found on the playground and my star-shaped eraser.

Sometimes I hold Grandma's hand or sit on her lap when she is getting her hair washed or when she has to take her medicine.

It's true that she's not the same person she used to be, but she's still my Grandma and I love her very much. She loves me too.

I can tell because she still remembers our special kiss.

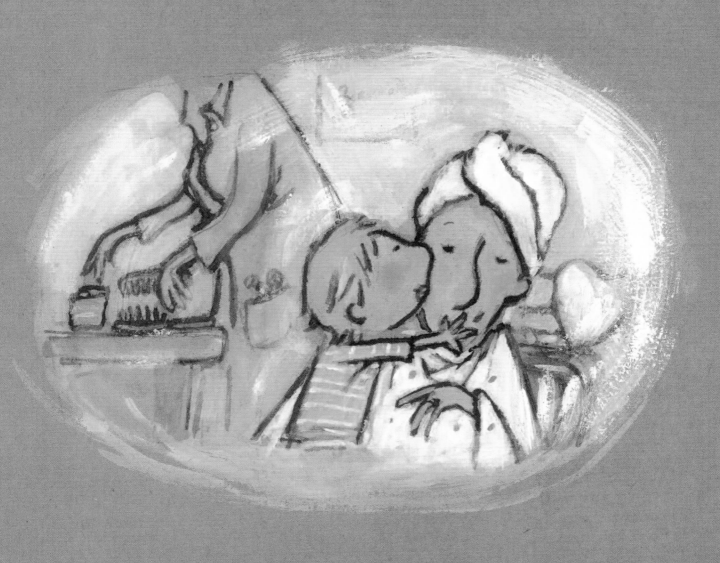